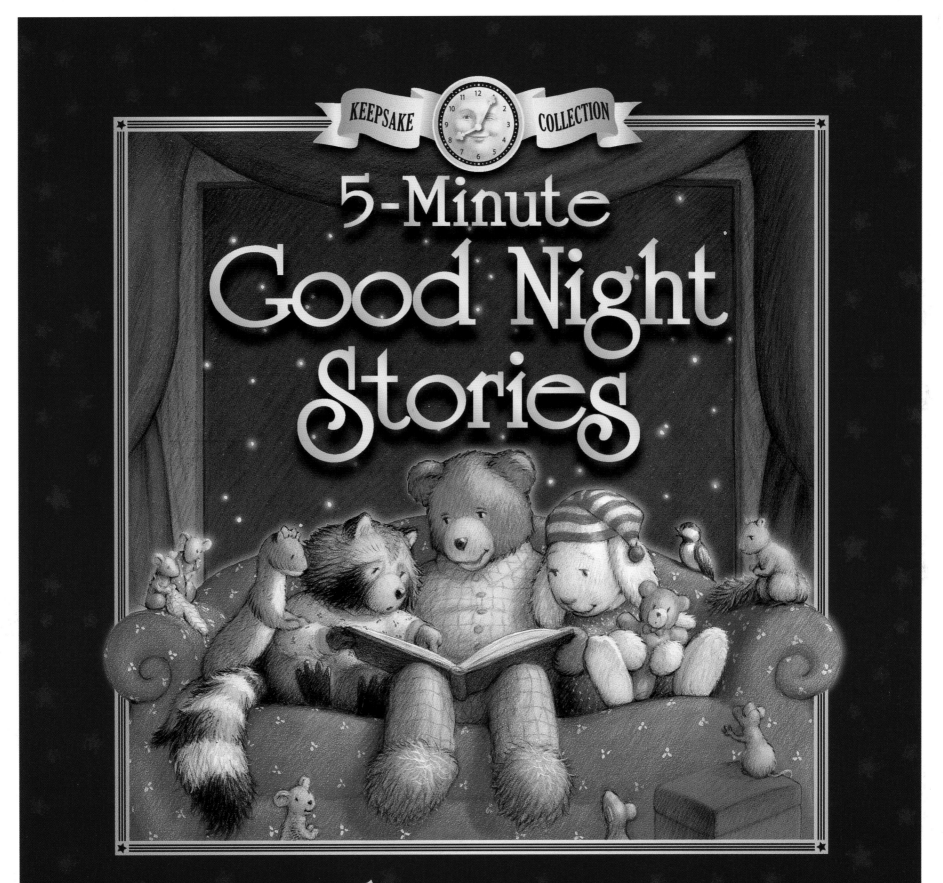

# 5-Minute Good Night Stories

KEEPSAKE COLLECTION

pi kids® publications international, ltd.

Cover and title page illustrated by Renée Graef

Louis Weber, C.E.O.
Publications International, Ltd.
7373 North Cicero Avenue
Lincolnwood, Illinois 60712

Ground Floor, 59 Gloucester Place
London W1U 8JJ

Customer Service: 1-800-595-8484 or customer_service@pilbooks.com

**www.pilbooks.com**

p i kids is a registered trademark of Publications International, Ltd.

Manufactured in China.

8 7 6 5 4 3 2 1

ISBN-13: 978-1-4127-6300-4
ISBN-10: 1-4127-6300-2

# 5-Minute Good Night Stories

KEEPSAKE COLLECTION

# Little Red Riding Hood

*Adapted by Michael P. Fertig*
*Illustrated by Wendy Edelson*

Once upon a time there was a playful little rabbit who always wore a bright red cloak with a hood. She wore her cloak every time she left the house. Everyone knew her as Little Red Riding Hood.

One day Little Red Riding Hood and her mother packed a basket full of good things to eat. Red Riding Hood was going to deliver the basket of goodies to Grandmother's house. They filled the basket with Grandmother's favorite foods. It was stuffed full of fresh carrots, orange-blossom honey, and several different homemade breads and tarts.

"Now please go straight to Grandmother's house," her mother said. "No dillydallying and no talking to strangers. Understand?"

Little Red Riding Hood nodded as her mother gave her a kiss on the forehead and sent her off through the woods to Grandmother's house.

Little Red Riding Hood hadn't gone far when a wolf leaped out from the trees. "Where are you going?" he asked curiously.

"I'm not to talk to strangers," said Little Red Riding Hood.

The wolf looked at her  basket. "Perhaps you're going on a picnic," he said. "You seem to have quite a few goodies packed away in that basket."

"It's not a picnic," said Little Red Riding Hood as she held the basket close. "This is for my grandmother. It has all her favorite things in it."

The wolf sniffed the basket. "No flowers? I would never visit my grandmother without a bunch of flowers. You should stop and pick some. You wouldn't want to let her down."

Little Red Riding Hood thought for a moment before deciding that this was a good idea. In fact, she was so busy picking flowers, she didn't even notice the wolf run off in the direction of Grandmother's pretty house.

Meanwhile, in her cottage, Grandmother was too distracted mending her apron to notice a great big, hairy wolf sneak into the house and into the wardrobe.

When the time was just right, the wolf took Grandmother by surprise.

"*GRRRRRAAAARRRRR*," snarled the wolf as he sprang from the wardrobe.

"Oh, my!" cried Grandmother. She couldn't believe what she was seeing.

"You look tasty," said the wolf.

Grandmother jumped up from her chair so quickly that she knocked the table right over. She ran out of that house as fast as she could.

The wolf, satisfied that Grandmother wouldn't be coming back anytime soon, looked through Grandmother's wardrobe and found her nightcap, gown, and some glasses. He put them on and leaped into bed.

The wolf nestled into Grandmother's big, comfortable bed and pulled the blankets right up over his nose. He closed his eyes, pretending to sleep soundly.

Little Red Riding Hood arrived a few minutes later. "Grandmother?" she called from the open door. "Grandmother, are you home?"

"I'm in here, my little dumpling," said the wolf softly.

Little Red Riding Hood hurried inside the house and headed straight for Grandmother's bedroom.

"Are you ill, Grandmother?" asked Little Red Riding Hood. "Why are you in bed? Mother sent me over with a basket full of your favorite things."

The wolf turned carefully to peek into the basket. As he shifted, Grandmother's nightcap fell from the wolf's head. Little Red Riding Hood seemed confused.

"Grandmother, what big ears you have," she said.

"All the better to hear you with," said the wolf, trying to disguise his voice.

Little Red Riding Hood thought her grandmother sounded funny, so she leaned in a little closer to hear better. When she got closer, Little Red Riding Hood noticed Grandmother's giant eyes.

"Grandmother, what big eyes you have," said Little Red Riding Hood.

"All the better to see you with," said the wolf.

Then the wolf slowly pulled down the covers, revealing his furry face.

"But Grandmother," said Little Red Riding Hood, "what big teeth you have!"

"All the better to *EAT* you with!" growled the wolf as he threw back the covers.

"You're not my grandmother!" shrieked Little Red Riding Hood. "Why, you're the big, bad wolf from the forest!"

"There's no reason to run," said the wolf as he bared his sharp teeth. "No one can help you."

"That's what you think," said a strong voice from behind them. Standing in the doorway were Grandmother and a big, strong lumberjack.

The wolf chuckled again. He didn't seem to be concerned at all.

"One old lumberjack can't catch a quick and smart wolf like me," bragged the wolf.

The wolf leaped toward the bedroom window, but Little Red Riding Hood grabbed the wolf's tail. Grandmother snatched up her nightcap from the bed and pulled it down over the wolf's eyes.

The lumberjack picked up the wolf and carried him off to the bank of the river. Little Red Riding Hood and her grandmother followed close behind.

The lumberjack set the wolf on a big log. He pushed the log into the water, and the wolf quickly sailed down the river.

"He doesn't look so big and scary in the middle of that wide river," said Grandmother.

"You sure are right, Grandmother," said Little Red Riding Hood. "He doesn't look so bad at all when he's so far away!"

"And even better than that, he doesn't look like he'll be coming back anytime soon," said the lumberjack as the wolf floated out of sight.

With the wolf safely gone, everyone went back to the house and enjoyed the food in the basket.

Little Red Riding Hood made many more trips through the forest to Grandmother's house after that, and was never again bothered by the big, bad wolf.

But Little Red Riding Hood did remember two things from her adventure that day. The first is that she should never, ever stop to talk to strangers. The second thing is that she should always remember to bring some flowers when she is going to visit her grandmother.

# Stone Soup

*Adapted by Lisa Harkrader*
*Illustrated by Barbara Lanza*

A traveling man walked along a dirt road. He had a feather in his hat and a smile on his face. His name was Jack Grand, and he would travel from one village to the next seeking to trade work for food. As it happened, Jack had been walking for a long time. It had been days since he'd been to a new village. He was hungry.

As Jack came over the top of a hill, he spied a town. This put a spring in Jack Grand's step.

"Where there is a village, there are people. Where there are people, there is work, and where there is work, there is food," he thought.

Jack ran to the village. He ran to the first house. A name was painted on the gate: TUBBS. He knocked on the door. An older man opened it. Jack swooped his hat from his head. He bowed low to the ground, then told his story to the man.

"I'm sorry," said Mr. Tubbs. "I have no food to share. I have only a bit of salt and pepper. Ask Miss Grubbs next door."

Jack hurried to the next house. He knocked on the door.

A thin woman answered. Jack swooped his hat from his head. He bowed low to the ground, then told his story.

"I'm sorry," said Miss Grubbs. "I have no food to share. I have only a head of garlic. You should ask Mrs. Chubbs next door."

Jack hurried to the next house. He knocked on the door.

A plump woman answered. Jack swooped his hat from his head. He bowed low to the ground, then told his story.

"I'm sorry," said Mrs. Chubbs. "I have no food to share. I have only a few

potatoes. I'm afraid you'll have to ask someone else."

Jack did. He knocked on every door in the village. He swooped his hat from his head. He bowed low to the ground, but nobody had enough food to share.

One woman only had a bit of cabbage, while her neighbor had only a few carrots. The family across the street had only a few slices of bacon, and another family up the road had only a handful of beans.

Jack sighed and set off down the road. He walked along for a while. He no longer had a smile on his face. He was too hungry to smile. He decided to sit down and rest.

As he sat, Jack spotted a stone.

This was not like the other stones in the road, however. It was smooth and white and round. Jack picked it up and was examining it when he was suddenly struck with an idea.

"Perfect," he said.

He was happy again. He was so happy he ran back to town. Once again he knocked on the first door in the village. Mr. Tubbs answered.

"I know you have no food to share," Jack said. "But I was hoping you might have a big cooking pot I could borrow."

As he spoke, Jack held up the smooth, white stone.

"What have you got there?" asked Mr. Tubbs.

"A soup stone," Jack said. "It makes great soup. I just add water. But first I need a great big soup pot."

Mr. Tubbs went inside. He came back with a big pot.

Jack carried the pot to the village square, filled it with water, and then built a fire underneath it. As Mr. Tubbs watched, Jack dropped the stone into the water.

The pot bubbled and brewed while Jack waited and waited as long as he could. Then he dipped his spoon into the water and tasted it.

"Perfect," he said.

"It's good?" asked Mr. Tubbs.

"Yes," said Jack. "It's very good. Only, well, I guess it would be better if…."

Mr. Tubbs leaned in closer.

"If what?" he asked.

"Well," said Jack, "it would probably be better with a little salt and pepper. Not much. Just a little. Oh, well. The soup will be just fine without it."

"I have salt and pepper," said Mr. Tubbs.

"You do?" said Jack.

"Yes!" said Mr. Tubbs.

He ran to his cottage as fast as he could. He came back with a salt shaker and a pepper mill.

Jack sprinkled the salt into the pot with a smile, then nodded at Mr. Tubbs as he ground the pepper into the pot. He stirred.

Miss Grubbs came out of her cottage. She had been watching Jack. She came over and peeked into the pot just as Jack tasted the soup.

"It's stone soup," said Mr. Tubbs.

"Is it good?" asked Miss Grubbs.

"Yes," said Jack. "It's very good. Except, I bet it might be even better if . . . ."

Miss Grubbs leaned in closer.

"If what?" she asked.

"Well," said Jack, "if it had a little garlic."

"Garlic?" Miss Grubbs asked. "I have garlic."

She ran to her cottage as fast as she could. She returned with a beautiful head of garlic.

Jack chopped the garlic and sprinkled it in.

"Perfect," he said.

Mrs. Chubbs came out of her cottage. She came over and peeked into the pot.

"It's stone soup," said Miss Grubbs.

"Is it good?" asked Mrs. Chubbs.

"Yes," said Jack. "It's very good. Only, it would probably be better if . . . ."

Mrs. Chubbs leaned in closer.

"If what?" she asked.

"Well," said Jack, "it would probably be better with a few potatoes. Not many, just a few. Oh, well. The soup will be just fine without them."

"Potatoes?" Mrs. Chubbs asked. "I have potatoes."

She ran to her cottage as fast as she could. She returned with her apron full of potatoes.

Jack peeled and sliced the potatoes and dropped the slices into the pot and stirred.

"Perfect," he said.

By this time, the entire village had gathered around Jack. They all wanted to know what was in the pot.

"It's stone soup," said Mrs. Chubbs.

"Is it good?" they asked.

"Yes," said Jack. "It's very good. But it just might be better if we had …."

"If we had what?" asked the villagers.

"Well, maybe some cabbage," said Jack. "Also, a few carrots might taste good, maybe a bit of bacon, perhaps some beans, but really, it should be just fine without those things."

A woman ran to get cabbage. A man ran to get carrots. All the villagers ran to get the food they had. Jack threw it all into the pot and stirred. The pot bubbled and brewed. Jack could hardly wait. He dipped his spoon into the soup and tasted it.

"Perfect," he said. "It's ready to eat."

Jack served the soup and everyone ate until the pot was empty. Empty, that is, except for the smooth, white stone.

"Use it for your next pot of stone soup," Jack said to the villagers.

With that, he waved good-bye to the villagers and set off.

He walked for a while. Then he sat down to rest. He saw a rock. It was shiny and black. He picked it up and put it in his pocket.

"It's perfect," he said, "for making rock stew."

# Bugville Bridge

*Written by Brian Conway*
*Illustrated by Richard Bernal*

Long ago, a few brave insects from the town of Bugville flew to a distant land they called Harvest Hill. There they found giant helpings of the finest foods! There was enough food in Harvest Hill to keep all the bugs in Bugville full for many, many years. As a matter of fact, the bugs had so much food that they decided to build a long bridge out of the leftovers. That way, the crawling bugs could get to Harvest Hill, too.

Construction on the Bugville bridge began immediately. Every type of food was used to make the bridge—cheese, licorice, and pickles, just to name a few.

The insects wasted little time, and in just days they had built their special bridge.

Before long, bugs were making the trip to Harvest Hill every day. They brought back loads of yummy treats with every trip, and everyone in Bugville was happy for a long time.

Bugville became the jolliest place around. The bugs had Banana Festivals every Tuesday, and Chocolate Carnivals three times a week. Every bug in Bugville ate ten meals a day, and many of them took naps in between meals.

Soon the worker bees were the only ones who made the long journey to Harvest Hill. The plump little bees would cross Bugville Bridge each day and bring back enough food for everybody. But over time, even the worker bees began to get lazy.

"I'm hungry," Benny Bee said as they crossed the bridge. "Let's stop for a snack."

Benny and Bessy Bee nibbled on the licorice that held the bridge together.

Just then, Gus Grasshopper walked by. He watched the lazy, hungry worker bees munch away on the food that held the bridge together. He shook his head as he said to himself, "This might be a problem."

Boy, was Gus right! It didn't take long for the other bugs to follow suit.

It seemed that everyone felt as though the bridge was a good place to have a snack. They would take a little nibble here and a little munch there, but no one thought to put any food back into the bridge. It wasn't long before the bridge simply crumbled down!

Lady Bug, the queen of Bugville, called for Gus. The queen knew that he'd be just the grasshopper to handle the job of rebuilding the bridge.

Queen Lady Bug brought out the plans and handed them over to Gus. "I'm counting on you to lead the crew to build a new bridge to Harvest Hill," she told him. "In fact, all of Bugville is counting on you."

Gus nodded. He was honored to take such an important job. He looked up at the queen and said, "We'll need carrots and celery and pretzels and cheese. I know I can help to make Bugville Bridge better than ever. But I'll need others to pitch in and lend a hand!"

With Queen Lady Bug's help, Gus Grasshopper spread the word around town. All the bugs were buzzing with excitement. Everyone would help build the new bridge.

The beetles and the caterpillars spent the whole day digging, while the dragonflies brought the longest, crispiest celery stalks back from Harvest Hill.

The ants were in charge of the pickle chips—no one
had to tell the ants how to get a whole lot of food from one place to another—while the
flies brought in fresh strands of licorice. Meanwhile, the centipedes
all got together to carry the pretzels back.

Queen Lady Bug was very pleased. She had never seen so
much activity in Bugville. It appeared as though every bug
was working on the bridge. But most of all, Queen Lady
Bug was thrilled to see all the insects working together.
"The mosquitoes are getting along with the moths,"
she told Gus, "and the termites are helping the earwigs!"
The resident insects of Bugville worked together
marvelously. The new bridge was looking fantastic.

1 9

At last the new Bugville Bridge was finished.

"Hurrah!" the bugs of Bugville buzzed.

Gus Grasshopper and Queen Lady Bug beamed with pride, too.

"The bridge looks great!" cheered Gus Grasshopper.

"It looks good enough to eat," Queen Lady Bug joked, but they all knew better than that.

This new bridge was even better than the last one. It was tall and strong and built to last.

And best of all, the bugs of Bugville did it together.

# The Brave Little Tailor

*Adapted by Michael P. Fertig*
*Illustrated by Jeremy Tugeau*

This is the story of a tailor. Unlike other stories about tailors that might be about sewing or stitching, this story is about how a tailor's ordinary life took a turn he never expected—thanks to the sweet fragrance of some raspberry jam.

It all began one morning while the tailor sat sewing a piece of red cloth at his breakfast table. He was just about to enjoy a sandwich with his favorite flavor of jam, when a swarm of seven flies came buzzing in his window.

The seven flies circled the jam jar and his bread. The tailor recognized the intentions of these unwanted visitors, and with a quickness that surprised even him, he lifted the red cloth above his head, and brought it down atop the table with a bang. The seven flies lay there motionless.

"Seven in one blow," said the tailor, amused at this accomplishment.

So amused was the tailor that he cut his red cloth into a belt, and as a reminder of his feat, he stitched "7 in one blow" right into the end of that belt.

Feeling jolly and just a little bit restless, the little tailor decided to take in the morning air. No sooner had he strolled over a hill in the meadow than he met a giant.

"Seven in one blow?" the giant said aloud as he read the little tailor's belt. He failed to realize, however, that the belt referred to seven flies. The giant thought that the tailor was bragging of defeating seven *men* with one blow.

"You must think you're pretty strong," said the giant.

"Seven men in one blow, eh? Well, if you're so strong, can you crush a rock like this?"

The giant plucked a huge boulder from the ground. He squeezed the boulder tight in his hand. The giant had crushed it so thoroughly, water dripped through his fingers!

The little tailor thought quickly and said, "Well, as you can see, I could not fit a boulder of such size into the palm of my hand, but I shall demonstrate with this instead." The tailor reached into his coat and pulled out a large hunk of cheese that he had brought to have as a snack. From the giant's great height, the cheese looked just like a rock. The tailor squeezed the cheese until milk dripped from his hand.

"You *do* have great strength," said the giant. "Please, come with me to meet my brothers and let us show you the hospitality you deserve."

The little tailor followed the giant home, where he was treated to a great feast of turkey legs, buttered bread, and mountains of mashed potatoes. Everyone became quite sleepy.

"You will sleep in this bed tonight," said the giant, pointing to a bed that was the size of a small castle. The tailor was much too uncomfortable sleeping in the middle of the bed, so he climbed way up into a corner of the giant mattress, where he was no more than a speck.

As it turned out, the giants were so afraid of the little tailor's strength, they sneaked into his room in the middle of the night. The giants began to beat the mattress with their clubs. The tailor, safely tucked away in the corner, made a mental note to remember this the next time a giant offered him a bed.

The next morning, the giant brothers went to the lake for their morning swim. They laughed about the little man and his silly belt. He wasn't so strong after all. But when the little tailor came walking to the edge of the water, the giant brothers became so afraid, they jumped out of the lake and ran for their lives without even stopping to take their clothes.

With a laugh, the tailor turned and began to walk. He walked for miles just enjoying the fresh air. As the morning turned to afternoon, and the afternoon turned to evening, the little tailor began to grow tired. He decided to relax under the setting sun and have a nap.

As he slept, two men from the king's army spotted the little tailor. They read the words on his belt. "Seven in one blow?" one of them said. The soldiers assumed that the little tailor was a great soldier himself, so they took him to meet their king.

The king read the tailor's sash. Like the giant, the king leapt to a conclusion. He assumed that the tailor had defeated seven *giants* with one blow.

"If a man is so proud of a feat that he decides to sew it into his clothing," said the king, "then to repeat such a feat should not be difficult for that man. I wonder, traveling soldier, will you capture me seven giants so I might behold this strength you possess?"

"My dear king," said the little tailor as he bowed, "you must understand that though this feat is indeed one that I could repeat, the mere act of finding seven giants together at the

same time is nearly impossible. I'm sure you understand."

"Very well," replied the king. "Then instead I will ask you only to disable two giants and capture me a wild unicorn."

Not having a choice, the little tailor set off into the forest with a hundred of the king's men. As they approached a clearing, the tailor stopped the men and told them to stand back—he must go in alone. The tailor had spotted two giants napping directly under a tree, and he had a plan.

Quickly and quietly, the tailor climbed the tall tree and began dropping acorns onto the heads of the giants.

The giants sat up and looked around. Seeing no one else, each thought the other had hit him over the head. They became so upset with one another that they fought until they both fell to the ground.

The tailor stood next to them and called for the soldiers. All one hundred of the king's men gawked as the little tailor stood there, casually picking a piece of lint off of his coat.

"If you wouldn't mind," the tailor said to the men, "perhaps you could bring these two giants to the king. And tell him I'll be by presently with his unicorn."

As the soldiers did this, the tailor tried to figure out how he was going to capture a wild unicorn. He didn't have to ponder long as he turned to see a wild unicorn charging right at him. The tailor stood perfectly still as the unicorn closed in on him. The tailor just dove out of the way as he heard a thud.

The tailor had been standing in front of a tree, and the unicorn had run smack into it, lodging its horn in the trunk. The little tailor freed the unicorn and rode it into the kingdom.

The king stood in awe. "You *are* a great soldier," the king said.

"Thank you, sir," said the little tailor. "It was quite easy, really. But not as easy as defeating seven in one blow."

# Saint George and the Dragon

*Adapted by Michael P. Fertig*
*Illustrated by Tammie Speer Lyon*

Once upon a time there lived a boy named George who was raised in the land of fairies. The fairies did their best to teach him right from wrong, and good from bad. They taught him to be a brave and noble knight.

Over time, George became very skilled with a sword. But what pleased his fairy guardians the most was that he was even more skilled with his mind.

Eventually the time came for George to go out into the world and seek his fate. The queen of fairies called him to see her.

"Your journey starts today," she told him. "You have many adventures before you."

"Yes, Your Majesty." George bowed before the queen. "I vow to make you proud." He was sad to leave, but he was not afraid.

George set off. As he traveled from village to village, he found himself faced with one challenge after another. As he walked, his mind wandered. He was so lost in thought that he didn't see the young woman standing before him until he was right upon her.

"Hello there," said George, trying to sound gallant. He noticed at once that the young woman looked distressed. "What is wrong, my lady? Is there anything I can do to help?"

"My name is Sabra," she said, "This is the village of Silene. I apologize for appearing so frantic, but I'm afraid our village is living at the mercy of an evil dragon."

George had heard countless stories of the hardships that had befallen the kingdom of Silene. He also remembered hearing stories about a brave and beautiful princess named Sabra. But he certainly never dreamed that he would actually meet her.

The princess told George why her kingdom lived in fear. Many months ago the dragon had risen high above the village walls. Until that day, Silene had been the picture of peace and happiness. Villagers would trade goods in the village square during the day, and at night they would all pitch in to create a great feast. They would dance and put on plays; it was a wonderful place to be — until the day that the dragon appeared.

"No one in the village even knew dragons still existed until this one arrived," said Sabra.

"The dragon surprised us all. Now he keeps the villagers captive inside the city walls. The dragon demands that he be given two sheep to eat each day, or he will eat the people for his dinner instead!"

George cringed at the thought of this.

"We gave up our last two sheep this morning," continued the princess. "Now we have nothing to give the dragon, and we shall all perish."

"What's more," she went on, "the dragon cannot be killed by sword alone; his scales are tougher than steel. Many men have already died trying to defeat him."

"Princess Sabra," said George, "may I ask where you were heading when I came across you earlier?"

"Oh, I almost forgot," she replied. "I had heard rumors of an old hermit who lives in a cave not far from the village. It is said that he is something of a prophet. I had hoped that he could provide some help."

George agreed that it might not hurt to see if this man could indeed help. Princess Sabra and George set off for the cave. The old man was sitting in the cave staring into a fire. His hair was whiter than snow, and his thick beard hung down to his belly.

George opened his mouth to speak, but before he could utter a word, he and Sabra were both startled by a small explosion at their feet. From out of nowhere appeared an hourglass. George and Sabra just stared.

It was then that the hermit finally spoke:

*"You both seek an answer,*
*I feel it from you twice.*
*The help you need is in this*
  *hourglass,*
*For it's filled with dragon ice."*

The pair stood quietly as the old man's voice echoed.

George and Sabra looked at each other. Dragon ice?

"I think we need to seek out the dragon now," said George.

George and Sabra arrived at the dragon's lair just as the dragon awoke from a deep slumber. As the dragon stretched and yawned a great, fiery yawn, George looked down at the hourglass. The last tiny grain of icy-looking sand was dropping. As soon as the grain touched the others, the hourglass glowed blue and became cold to the touch.

George instantly knew what had to be done. He threw the hourglass at the dragon's open mouth. It shattered on the dragon's tongue in a great cloud of icy mist. The icy sand froze the dragon's mouth shut. The crystals in the hourglass spread to the dragon's stomach and began to freeze the beast from the inside out. The dragon's greatest weapon, the fire which grew from the oven of his belly, was destroyed!

The dragon had no choice but to live out his years in the depths of the warm spring in his cave. George and Sabra had saved the kingdom from the terrors of the dragon.

Sabra offered George a large reward. He turned it down.

"My reward is knowing that your village is safe," he said.

With that, George continued on in his journey. His selfless attitude and desire to help are two of the reasons he is still remembered as a saint today.

# The Boy Who Cried Wolf

*Adapted by Jennifer Boudart*
*Illustrated by Jon Goodell*

The village of Woolington was known for sheep. Everybody had at least one. The doctor, the butcher, the blacksmith, and the mayor all had sheep.

What was so great about Woolington sheep? Their wool, of course! The town held a wool sale every spring. Buyers came from near and far.

There was no question about it—Woolington loved its sheep. No one in Woolington loved them more than Timothy the shepherd boy.

Timothy took his job very seriously. Each day, he gathered the town's sheep, walked them down the street, and herded them into the meadow. Timothy found the greenest grass and the coolest water for the sheep. He pulled rocks from their hooves and he combed their wool. Woolington was very proud of Timothy.

"Timothy is a terrific shepherd," said the town doctor.

"Timothy treats those sheep like family," said the butcher.

"Timothy always keeps the sheep safe," said the blacksmith.

Timothy's father had taught him the first rule of being a shepherd: "A shepherd boy must keep his sheep safe." This was something Timothy always remembered.

While he was on the job, Timothy never took a nap. He never read a book. He only watched for trouble. Maybe he did daydream a little, but he never had any real trouble. A lamb might try to run away, a dog might scare the sheep, or one of them might get its foot stuck in a hole. Those were small things.

"Watch out for wolves," Timothy's father had said.

But Timothy had never seen a wolf in the meadow. He had never seen a wolf anywhere.

From the meadow, Timothy could clearly see Woolington. He watched all the children play in the village and realized that he was bored. Timothy wanted to play like the other children.

As he sat and daydreamed, he began to wonder what he would do if a wolf came along. He was just a small boy; a wolf would not be scared off by him. In fact, it was Timothy who would be afraid of the wolf.

What would he do? He could call for help, that's what.

The people of Woolington would hear him. He had a very loud voice. Everyone would run down the street and rush into the meadow, and the wolf would run away.

Timothy stood up. What if he pretended to see a wolf? Would the people of Woolington come running? That would be exciting. A little excitement was just what he needed.

"Help! Help!" Timothy yelled. "A wolf is after the sheep!"

It wasn't true. All the sheep were there. They were eating grass. They didn't even notice when he ran behind a tree.

Timothy watched people run from their shops and homes.

"Timothy needs help!" the people said. Everyone ran to the meadow. The Woolington sheep were in trouble. Their shepherd boy was in trouble! They all rushed up the hill to help young Timothy. But all the sheep were there. The people of Woolington were confused.

"What is this?" asked the doctor. "Where's Timothy?"

"I don't see a wolf at all!" said the butcher.

"The only thing out of place is Timothy," said the confused blacksmith.

"Maybe the wolf dragged him away!" said the mayor.

Everyone got nervous.

Everyone started shouting and running again. They looked for wolf tracks and any sign of Timothy. One boy spotted Timothy's crook next to a big tree. He ran to grab it.

"Timothy is here," he said.

Everyone looked at the big tree. Timothy came out from behind it, took a few steps, and fell over with laughter.

"Do you think this is funny?" said the mayor. "We were scared! But now we're just angry. Making up stories about wolves is not funny. Do not play tricks like that again."

Timothy tried to say he was sorry but his giggles got in the way.

When Timothy got home, there was big trouble. His father was angry.

"I didn't want to upset anyone," Timothy said. "But it was a good test. I wanted to know what would happen if there was a wolf."

Timothy also thought it had been very funny. But he didn't say that.

Timothy collected the sheep the next day. People were still angry.

"I worry about these sheep every day," he said to himself. "It would be nice for people to worry about *me* for once."

Timothy was angry that nobody worried about him. He was so angry that he made a decision. He led the sheep to the meadow—then he started yelling.

"Help!" he yelled. "A real wolf has come! He is after the sheep!"

Timothy found another place to hide as the townspeople came running. They knew right away that they had been tricked.

"Come out, Timothy," said the mayor. "You let us down. We told you not to play tricks but you didn't listen. Maybe next time we won't believe you if you call for help."

Timothy felt bad. The mayor was right. He had been doing more than playing tricks—he had been telling lies.

A few days passed. Timothy took extra good care of the sheep. He wanted to prove he was still a good shepherd.

He sat and watched for trouble. Then Timothy heard a strange noise come from one of the sheep. It wasn't the kind of noise a sheep should make.

A wolf was in the meadow! It was chasing the Woolington sheep. Timothy could see its sharp teeth.

"Help! Help!" Timothy yelled. "A wolf is in the meadow! It's chasing the sheep!"

Timothy watched and waited for someone to come running. No one came. Timothy called for help again.

"A real wolf has come!" he yelled. "I am not making it up! I need help!"

Timothy was shouting as loud as he could. No one even looked at him. Timothy could hear the wolf growling. He shook his crook at the wolf.

The wolf was not afraid.

"Someone please help me!" he yelled. Still, no one came.

Timothy was very afraid. He ran all the way to Woolington.

"A wolf is in the meadow!" he said.

"Stop your tricks, Timothy," they all said.

When Timothy tried to talk to the mayor, he just walked away.

"I am telling the truth!" Timothy yelled. No one paid attention. No one believed him.

Timothy remembered the mayor's warning.

"Maybe next time we won't believe you if you call for help," he had said. If only Timothy had not played tricks!

He ran back to the meadow. The wolf was gone. The Woolington sheep were gone, too. The wolf had taken them all away. Timothy had broken the first rule: He had not kept the sheep safe. Timothy was sorry about what happened.

Not a day goes by now when Timothy doesn't wish he hadn't cried wolf. He learned a very difficult lesson that day. He learned that if you want to be trusted, you must always be honest.

# Robin Hood

*Adapted by Michael P. Fertig*
*Illustrated by Marty Noble and Muriel Wood*

At the young age of fifteen, there was a boy living in Sherwood forest who could handle a bow and arrow better than any grown man in the village of Nottingham. This boy, named Robin Hood, had one wish, and that was to become a member of the king's Foresters. The Foresters were a group of men that policed the forest on behalf of the king. Robin felt that this was a noble job. At least, that's what he thought until he approached the Sheriff of Nottingham. Robin was certain that he'd be hired on the spot. After all, no one could use a bow and arrow as well as he could.

The sheriff just laughed at Robin. When Robin protested, the sheriff tried to arrest him.

If it hadn't been for the friends that Robin Hood had made in Sherwood Forest, he would certainly have been taken prisoner.

It was with these friends that Robin Hood formed a band of men who lived together in the forest. They became known as the Merry Men. The sheriff learned that Robin and his Merry Men would rob rich civilians who passed through the forest. But what made the sheriff really angry was that Robin would give the money to the poor.

The sheriff hatched a plan to catch Robin Hood.

"Men," called Robin to his friends, "I've just heard that the sheriff is holding an archery contest. And I intend to win!"

"But Robin," cried Little John, the largest man in the group, "everyone knows you're the greatest archer this side of the sky. Surely this must be some sort of trap!"

"Ah, Little John," said Robin with a smile, "wise you are. I suspect the very same thing. Therefore we shall attend the contest in disguise."

That night they set about getting their costumes in order. Robin decided he would dress as a one-eyed beggar. He fashioned an eye patch and dressed in rags. He even dyed his hair and beard a lighter color to be sure he wouldn't be recognized.

Robin and his Merry Men arrived in Nottingham's town square to find it packed. The square was also swarming with the sheriff's men.

As he expected, Robin sailed through the first several rounds of the competition. He won every match. Soon he was in the final competition against an accomplished archer called Hugh o' the Moors.

Hugh was very good. The match came down to one final shot. Hugh o' the Moors released a perfect arrow that hit the exact center of the target. The crowd reacted with a loud cheer. It would take a miracle to beat that shot.

The one-eyed beggar stood poised and ready. The crowd looked on nervously as they saw a small grin creep across the archer's face. He released his arrow and began to bow almost before the arrow reached its target. The crowd gasped as they tried to comprehend what they had just witnessed. The beggar's shot was so perfect and true, it actually split Hugh o' the Moor's arrow in half. The beggar had won the competition. The silent crowd suddenly stood and exploded into cheers!

The Sheriff of Nottingham, having given up on finding Robin Hood, approached the beggar and his circle of friends at once. He awarded the beggar his prize.

"My friend," said the sheriff, "that was as good an exhibition of an archer's skill as anyone is likely to ever see. Not even that filthy outlaw Robin Hood could have beaten that. I insist that you join me for a celebration feast at my home."

Robin tried to hide his laughter. "It would be my pleasure, Sheriff," he said. "May I impose to invite my friends as well? It wouldn't be a celebration without them."

"Of course," said the sheriff. "In fact, I insist."

Robin Hood and his Merry Men followed the sheriff to his home. That night Robin and his men enjoyed the sheriff's food and drink. They stayed late into the night and took turns sneaking off to other rooms in the sheriff's home to steal anything of value they could find. As the night wore down, Robin and his men bid the sheriff good night.

The sheriff smiled while thinking about the enjoyable night he had just spent with the winner of his archery contest. At the very moment the sheriff leaned to blow out a candle

for the night, an arrow whizzed by his ear, lodging itself into the painting that hung just inches from his head. The sheriff saw a note hanging from the arrow.

The sheriff felt a sick feeling sneak into his belly as he read the note out loud: "Sheriff, it was Robin Hood who won the contest and dined at your home this night. And it was the Merry Men who stole so many of your possessions while you gave them food and drink. Thank you for the evening."

For many months, the sheriff tried in vain to capture the elusive Robin Hood.

One day Robin was in a fresh disguise, working in the village of Nottingham peddling pots for a potter who lacked the energy to do so on his own. Robin was very charming and sold every one of the potter's pots, earning a pretty penny for the old man.

One of the villagers who happened to take a shine to Robin was the wife of the sheriff. So touched was she by Robin's caring nature that she invited him to dinner that night. Robin graciously accepted.

Before heading to the sheriff's for dinner, Robin gathered his Merry Men in the forest. He had a plan.

If this worked, the sheriff would surely double his efforts to catch Robin Hood and all of his men. Robin arrived at the sheriff's home in his potter disguise. The sheriff and his wife were very gracious, serving a wonderful feast. Not long into dessert, however, the conversation turned to Robin Hood. The sheriff noted his hatred for the outlaw. He particularly hated that everyone loved him.

"I wish I had known of your distaste for that villain, Sheriff," said Robin Hood. "For just this morning I myself shot and wounded him with my very own arrow. In fact, I have his bow outside on my horse."

Not believing what he heard, the sheriff followed the man outside. Sure enough, he had the most beautiful archer's bow known to Nottingham. It was Robin Hood's, all right.

"He's wounded, you say?" said the sheriff. "You must take me to him at once."

Robin and the sheriff rode side by side into Sherwood Forest. As they reached a clearing and jumped down from their horses, Robin pulled a horn out from under his cape and blew. The sound was a signal to his men, and in no time, the sheriff found himself surrounded.

"I'm afraid you've been duped again, Sheriff," said Robin Hood.

They robbed the sheriff, giving a satchel of gold to the old potter. The next day they would give the rest of the gold to the poor people of Nottingham.

Tonight, however, Robin and his men enjoyed their victory over the sheriff with a great feast. The war wasn't over, but Robin and his men had won this battle.

# The Little Dutch Boy

*Adapted by Brian Conway*
*Illustrated by Linda Dockey Graves*

Once there was a little Dutch boy named Hans. The town Hans lived in was next to the sea, so the farmers who lived there built big walls around their farms. The big walls, called dikes, kept the sea from flooding the farms.

Hans was a regular boy. He went to school with the other children in town. He played with his friends after school. He did his chores.

"Hans," his mother said, "I need you to take this basket of food to Mr. Van Notten."

Mr. Van Notten was an old friend of theirs. He lived on a farm on the edge of town.

"You are a good boy, Hans," his mother said. "I will have dinner waiting for you."

Hans set off on the main road out of town. He passed the town's main dike as he walked. Hans was lost in thought and arrived at Mr. Van Notten's house before he knew it.

"My dear friend!" Mr. Van Notten said. "I am so glad to see you!"

Hans smiled and shook Mr. Van Notten's hand as he gave him the basket.

"Look at all of these wonderful things," Mr. Van Notten said. "Come inside. We will have a bite to eat."

Hans stayed for a cup of cocoa. He also stayed for a few stories. Mr. Van Notten told the best stories. Hans's favorite stories were about when Mr. Van Notten was a small boy growing up in this little town. He had watched them build the big dikes that protected the city and its farms. Hans thought it was neat that Mr. Van Notten was as old as the dikes.

Hans glanced outside and realized that he had lost track of time.

"Oh, no! It's getting dark," he said. "I really must be getting home."

"It looks like a storm is coming," Mr. Van Notten said. "Hurry home!"

Hans walked up the road. He felt a few cold raindrops fall. The wind began to blow as the sky became very dark.

Hans pulled his hat down over his ears. The rain came down in sheets. Hans was soaked and every gust of cold wind made him walk faster and faster.

The storm grew worse with every step. The strong wind made the trees bend low. It blew the cold rain into Hans's eyes. He walked into the wind and with each step he slipped and slid along the muddy road. The wind knocked him back and spun him around. He could hardly see a thing in front of him until he finally spotted the dike.

"Thank goodness," he said. "I am almost home."

He went over to the dike, knowing he could use it to lead himself back home. But something about the dike was not right. Though it was raining buckets, there was more water on the ground than there should have been. That's when Hans noticed that seawater gushed from the stones. There was a crack in the wall. The dike had sprung a leak!

Hans ran toward town. He felt his way along the dike through the storm. He hurried as fast as he could go.

"I must get to town and warn the others," he thought.

Hans never thought the dike could break. It was the strongest thing he knew. The dike had stood up to many fierce storms. Strong winds and crashing waves had never harmed it. The dike kept the little town safe.

Hans arrived in town at last. The streets were dark and empty.

"The dike is leaking!" he shouted.

There was terrible thunder and howling winds. No one could hear him.

"We are in danger!" he shouted, but his voice was nothing more than a squeak. The storm was too loud.

Hans did not see anyone. Every house was closed up. Every door was bolted shut. Every window was sealed.

"Somebody help!" Hans shouted, but nobody heard him.

"There is no one to help me," he thought. "I will have to fix the dike."

Hans knew nothing about mending walls. Besides, he had no tools and no supplies. He ran back to the crack in the dike. The crack had grown bigger!

Hans looked around for something he might use to fix it. He found some branches and put them into the crack, but the seawater just squirted around them. So he dug up a handful of mud and put it into the crack. The seawater washed it away.

Hans was scared. He could hear waves pounding against the stone wall. The crack in the dike became a little bigger with every crash. The storm was not settling down.

"I have to do something," he thought.

There was nothing left to plug the hole. Hans balled up his fist and pushed it into the hole. The steady stream of cold water around it slowed down. Just a few drops fell from the crack.

Hans had plugged up the hole. But how long could he hold back the sea? He tried not to think about that. He tried to be proud of his cleverness. He tried to feel strong.

As Hans stood at the dike, moments became hours. The rain and winds became colder. Hans wondered if his mother would send someone to find him.

Hans's mother was very worried. She had been waiting for Hans for a very long time. It was the middle of the night.

"Oh, Hans," she said, "Where are you?"

She closed the window. She hoped that Hans had kept out of the storm. She hoped he had stayed in the safety of Mr. Van Notten's house. No one could survive outside during such a storm.

The storm settled down the next morning. Hans did not notice when the sun came up. He shivered with cold. His legs were exhausted.

Mr. Van Notten had worried all night about Hans. He wondered if Hans had made it home. He wanted to be sure. He called for his old dog and they walked toward town.

As Mr. Van Notten neared the dike, he squinted and saw a familiar shape. Was that Hans? His young friend was holding back the sea with his little hand.

Hans sniffled and yawned, still shivering. He looked up to see Mr. Van Notten.

"My dear friend!" Mr. Van Notten said. "You are a hero. You've saved the town from a horrible flood."

Hans looked up with a weak smile.

Mr. Van Notten hurried up the road to get help. In no time, a group of people arrived. They brought tools and supplies to repair the dike, and they brought dry blankets for Hans. They carried him home to his mother. She was very happy to see him. She warmed his face with kisses.

The doctor arrived to check on Hans, who was tucked into his warm, dry bed. He had the sniffles, but he would be okay. More importantly, though, he was safe.

"My brave little boy," his mother said. "You saved us all."

Everyone heard about what Hans had done. They were proud of him.

The mayor called all the townspeople together.

"Hans worked through the night to hold back the flood," he said. "He saved us all while we were asleep. While he is sleeping, we must return the favor and prepare a celebration for him."

Hans woke up to the sound of a band playing. He peeked out of his bedroom window. He saw every person from town in the street below. There was also a huge band, tents with food, and beautiful decorations. All the faces in the crowd looked up at him and cheered.

The mayor presented Hans with a medal of honor. The little Dutch boy was a hero. Even after Hans was all grown up, everyone still called him the boy who saved the town.

# Black Beauty

*Adapted by Michael P. Fertig*
*Illustrated by Jon Goodell*

See those two horses in the picture down there? The little one is me. That's my mom with me. I was just a young colt back then. I remember those days well. Mom and I would spend every day together, running around the green meadow and eating our fill of the delicious grass that grew there. I loved that farm. I also loved the days when my mom taught me things that would be important as I got older.

"Pay attention to what I'm about to say," she told me once. "The other colts you play with are very nice but they have not learned their manners. To have manners you must be gentle and good, and do your work with a good will."

Mom would always give me good advice, and I tried my hardest to follow it.

As I got older, I heard men talk about how I had grown to become a fine horse. I was kept on the same farm until I was four years old. By that time I had been taught to carry people and pull carts.

It was about then that I learned I was being sold. I didn't know whether this was good or bad, as I'd never left my farm before. I was sad to go, but excited to see what new adventures awaited me. At first things weren't so bad, but eventually, life got pretty rough for me. But I'll get to that in a little bit.

I was sold to an estate called Birtwick Park. It was a beautiful place. There were many other horses in the stable with me, and the trainers were very nice. The owners of the house would take each of us out for daily rides around the grounds. It was pleasant work.

I grew especially fond of the stable boy, Joe Green. He seemed to like me, too. Joe was in charge of putting up all the horses for the night. But he always seemed to pay extra attention to me.

The time I spent at Birtwick Park was wonderful. But I remember one night in particular that was not so wonderful. In fact, it was scary.

Late one night, I was asleep in my stall when the stable doors flew open. Joe Green and the head horse trainer, John Manley, came rushing in. John was telling Joe that the lady of the house, Mrs. Gordon, was very sick. If the doctor didn't get to the house immediately, Mrs. Gordon could die.

They opened my stall and led me out of the stable. I was fitted with my harness and saddle. John Manley hopped up onto my back, flicked the reins on my harness, and we were off. I ran as hard and as fast as I could. In no time we arrived at the doctor's.

John Manley leaped from my back and sprang to the door.

"Mrs. Gordon is desperately ill," said John. "We fear that she won't make it through the night if you cannot get there at once."

The doctor gathered his things then hopped on my back. I ran even faster on the return trip. I ran harder than I ever had before. I ran right up the path to the front of the house. The doctor rushed in the front door to tend to Mrs. Gordon. Joe Green was waiting for me. I was sweating and breathing hard. Joe Green looked at me with concern. As it turned out, Mrs. Gordon wasn't the only one to fall ill; apparently, so had I.

I was too weak to stand or eat. Joe Green slept in the stall with me, taking care of me. I knew I would recover.

In no time I was as good as new. Thankfully, so was Mrs. Gordon. But the doctor recommended that she move to a warmer climate to help her recovery. As I watched her ride off in her carriage, I couldn't help but think that a change was coming.

As it turned out, Mrs. Gordon's move would mark the beginning of a very difficult time in my life. I had been lucky so far, but my luck was about to change.

I was sold to a man who needed a horse to pull a delivery cart. I would begin at the crack of dawn, and pull a cart that was positively huge and overloaded. I would drag it up steep hills, across vast meadows, through wide rivers and creeks, and over rocky roads.

I thought I was lucky when he decided to sell me. But luck wasn't on my side this time, either. I was bought by a man who ran a carriage company. It wasn't bad at first, but I soon realized that this man would sometimes make his horses pull carriages for days straight without a rest. It was backbreaking work.

As a result, this man's horses grew weak very quickly, and he was forced to sell them. I was sold a number of times after that. Each time I kept hoping that one of my masters would treat me better. But it never happened.

I was sent from horse market to horse market. I was starting to think I belonged with the old horses that were too worn-out to work anymore.

It was at one of these markets that my life took an amazing turn. A young boy convinced his grandfather to buy me. "We can make him strong again, Grandpapa," the boy said. "We can make him strong like we did with Ladybird."

Grandpapa looked me over and said, "I think you're right, Willie. This is a fine horse."

They bought me and took me home. Their farm was lovely, and Willie treated me like a king's horse. But no sooner did I get used to it than it was time to move again.

"I have some news, Willie," Grandpapa said. "You've done such a good job of making this fine horse healthy and strong again, that I've found a new owner for him."

Willie was sad to hear this, and so was I, but Grandpapa assured him that I would be happier than I had ever been before.

I was taken to my new home the next day. Something seemed familiar about it as we trotted up the path. Three well-dressed ladies came out and smiled at Grandpapa as I heard a voice from near the stables.

"I don't believe it!" the voice yelled. I looked over and saw a figure running toward us, still yelling. "Could it be true?"

I was confused until one of the well-dressed women said, "Joe Green, what's all this fuss about? What is it that you cannot believe?"

"This is Black Beauty, ma'am!" he said. "He's been brought back to us!"

Grandpapa was right: I *was* happier than I had ever been before.

# Rip Van Winkle

*Adapted by Michael P. Fertig*
*Illustrated by John Lund*

The Catskill Mountains are a magical place—a place filled with legends. Those that live in and near the mountains have been passing these legends down over the years. There are some truly amazing stories that almost seem too strange to be true.

One such story is about a man named Rip Van Winkle. Rip lived in a village at the foot of the mountains. He was one of the friendliest people in the village, strolling through the town square, greeting everyone he saw with a wave and tip of his cap. In fact, Rip would never turn down someone who asked for help. He regularly helped others with their chores.

Rip's only fault was that he did not like to do his own chores. This bothered his wife.

"I thought you were going to fix the fence today," she said.

"It's a very big fence," Rip replied.

He decided that the fence could wait until tomorrow. He called for his dog, Wolf, then he smiled and waved at his children, Rip Jr. and Judy, and headed for the mountains.

Rip and his dog spent a lot of time in the mountains. Some days they'd just sit and enjoy the view. Today was one of those days.

Rip leaned against a tree as he stared out over the valley. As he relaxed, he heard some rustling coming from a bush nearby. Rip turned around to see an odd little man carrying a huge barrel on his shoulder.

"Would you help me with this?" the little man asked. The little man was strange, but Rip could not refuse anyone who asked for help.

"Of course," Rip said. "I'd love to help."

He took the barrel from the strange little man and climbed up the mountain after him. As they climbed, Rip heard loud claps and crashes that sounded like thunder. Rip looked around but there was not a cloud in the sky.

The little man smiled as he led Rip through a crack in a cliff and into a clearing.

Rip just stared as they walked into the clearing. A group of strange little men were gathered there. Rip saw something even more unusual as they got closer. The strange little men were bowling. Every time the ball hit the pins, there was a crash. The sound echoed through the mountains. It sounded like thunder!

Rip watched the men for a moment before the others noticed him. He had never seen such a sight in these hills before, and he had taken many strolls up here over the years.

It was then that the little bowlers saw Rip. One of them took the barrel from him. He poured a dark liquid from it, filling cups for all the little men.

The little men offered a cup to Rip. He drank the dark liquid. It was delicious. He asked for more. Rip drank several cups and started to feel tired. His eyes drooped and his head felt heavy. He drifted off to sleep.

Rip awoke with a start. He looked around, remembering where he was. Judging from the way the sun hung in the sky, Rip could tell it was morning again.

"I have been here all night," he said. "Mrs. Van Winkle is going to be very upset."

He whistled for his dog. Wolf did not come running.

"Maybe Wolf ran home," he said. "I should do the same thing."

Rip walked down the mountainside as he remembered the dream he had about the strange little men. Or was it a dream? It seemed pretty real. Anyway, Rip forgot all about the dream as he walked into town. The people he saw did not look familiar. He didn't seem to know anyone, and they didn't seem to know him. In fact, almost all of the townspeople stared at Rip. He smiled. He waved. He tipped his hat. Some of the people laughed. Others looked the other way. What was going on?

Finally, Rip looked down. He saw why everyone had been staring at him. He had a long gray beard!

Rip was more confused than ever.

"I'd better get home," Rip said. "Things will be all right once I see my wife and children."

But Rip got lost on the way to his house. The paths and roads were no longer the same.

After some time, Rip found his farmhouse. It did not look at all like it did the day before. The fence had fallen to the ground, weeds grew all over, and the roof was falling in. He walked slowly toward the house. It was dark and dirty inside. It was clear that nobody had lived there in a very long time. What had happened to his family? Where were his wife and kids?

In a panic, Rip ran back to town. He wanted to find something familiar. He needed to find someone who knew him.

Rip walked to the one place where he knew he could always find his friends — the inn. But the inn was not where it used to be. There was a schoolhouse there instead.

A man dressed in a fine suit walked up to Rip.

"Can I help you?" he asked.

"I am looking for someone who remembers me," Rip said. "My name is Rip Van Winkle."

"Rip Van Winkle?" the man asked. "I know Rip, and you're not him. That's Rip Van Winkle over there."

The man pointed to a tree. Beneath the tree stood a young man. The man looked just like Rip had yesterday.

Rip didn't respond. He simply stared at the man under the tree. His mind raced. He was starting to believe that his nap in the mountains had lasted a bit longer than he thought.

Just then, a woman and her children walked over to Rip.

"Hello," she said said. "I'm so sorry to bother you, but my name is Judy Gardener. I was just wondering if I look familiar to you, because you look familiar to me."

Rip leaned forward to look at Judy's face. There *was* something familiar about her.

"What is your father's name?" Rip asked her.

"Rip Van Winkle," she said. "But I haven't seen him in twenty years. He walked up into the mountains one day and he never came back. His dog came home without him."

The woman began to cry softly. "And what about your mother?" Rip asked.

"She passed away a few months ago," Judy said. Rip began to cry, too. His wife was gone. His children had grown. He had missed twenty years of his life!

"Are you all right, sir?" Judy asked.

"Please don't call me sir," Rip said. "Don't you recognize me? Don't you know who I am? I am Rip Van Winkle! I am your father!"

The woman and young man just stared. How could they believe this?

"I fell asleep on the mountain," he said. "Now everything has changed. Doesn't anyone know me?"

Young Rip, always his father's son, wanted to help. He went to find the tailor's wife. She was the oldest woman in town. If she did not know the stranger, nobody would.

The old woman looked into old Rip's eyes. She squinted.

"Sure enough," she said. "I'd know him anywhere. Welcome home, Rip Van Winkle."

Rip smiled, sad but relieved. He told his family about the little men, the clearing in the mountains, the strange liquid he drank, and his long nap.

"When I woke up," he said, "it was twenty years later! My life passed by in one night!"

It was not easy for Rip to accept what had happened to him, but in time, he became fond of telling people his story. His story became a legend and townsfolk would regularly gather around Rip's chair to listen.

To this day, the sound of thunder in the Catskill Mountains makes people talk. They say it is Rip's strange little friends bowling on the mountaintops.

# Prince Carrots

*Adapted by Jamie Elder*
*Illustrated by Kathy Mitchell*

Although it may not be very nice to talk about, there are some people who are born with faces that only their mothers could love. Such a boy was born, many years ago, to a young king and queen. His parents were quite handsome, but apparently good looks weren't one of the things that ran in the family.

You see, this prince was not very handsome. In fact, he was very hard to look at. His face was too wide, his nose was too long, his mouth was much too big, and he had bright orange hair. It was on account of his hair that he came to be called Prince Carrots.

The queen was upset about the way he looked, and her best friend, Mercury the Magician, could tell.

"You must not worry," he said. "The prince will be very intelligent. People will love him for it."

"Can you make him handsome?" she asked.

"No," he said. "I cannot make him what he is not."

After a pause, Mercury added, "I *can* give him a special gift. He will have the ability to give his intelligence to the person he loves the most."

The queen felt a little better. She loved her son dearly, and though she tried not to look away from him, every year was worse.

Regardless of the awkward color of his hair, or the bulging of his eyes, he was still very intelligent. People always asked him questions and he always had the answers.

His father would quiz him about naval strategy. Prince Carrots would demonstrate his knowledge using models. This impressed his father.

Prince Carrots's mother would ask him to tell her about the Trojan War. It was one of her favorite stories.

"Well," the prince would begin, "Helen of Troy was kidnapped because she was so beautiful. And because she was so beautiful, the Greeks went to war to save her."

In addition to being very intelligent, Prince Carrots was also surprisingly funny. He knew great jokes, and at parties he would often find himself surrounded by the guests. It was at one of these parties that his great big eyes spotted the most beautiful woman he had ever seen.

He recognized her as a princess from a neighboring kingdom. She was simply breathtaking. Prince Carrots could not look away. He walked straight to her. With a shy smile, he introduced himself.

"I am Prince Carrots," he said.

"I am Princess Pia," she said.

"I am honored to meet you," he said.

"It is *I* who am honored," she replied.

"Really?" he asked. "You are?"

The prince was shocked. Princesses would usually just stare at him. No princess had ever been *honored* to meet him.

"Yes," she said. "You are very smart. I have been told that you are smart. I have been told more than a thousand times."

Still, she did not smile. The prince knew there was a reason. His face made people look away, but it did not make them sad. This princess was sad. So Prince Carrots sat down next to her. He told her a joke, but she did not laugh. She just looked at him with blank eyes. She did not understand his joke.

"Why are you so unhappy?" he asked her.

"I am not sure why," she said. "I only know that I am stupid."

"But you are very beautiful," he said. "Surely you're joking about being stupid."

"No," she said. "I know I'm beautiful, but I also know I'm stupid. I was born that way. I've been told this more than a thousand times."

Pia told Prince Carrots a story.

"My mother has a friend," the princess said. "He is a magician. When I was young, mother told him she was worried about me. I was beautiful, but I was not very smart. My mother wanted him to make me more intelligent, but he told her he couldn't. He said he couldn't make me something that I was not. But he told her not to worry because I would be loved for my beauty."

The prince nodded when he heard that.

"The magician told her he would give me a gift, however," Princess Pia continued. "He said I would be able to give my beauty to someone—to the person I loved most."

The prince nodded again. Mercury had given him a similar gift. The princess found

the prince to be a good listener. But he was hard to look at. When she looked away, he did not seem to mind. She especially liked that he smiled a lot; it made her happy.

Prince Carrots and Princess Pia had fallen in love with each other. They spent all their time together, but things were different, things were strange.

"Did I ever tell you about the Trojan War?" he asked.

"Oh, yes," the princess said. "The Greeks rescued Helen because she was so beautiful."

Of course he had told her about the Trojan War! The funny thing was, he could not remember doing so.

"Did I tell you what happened at breakfast?" the princess asked.

"No," the prince said. "What happened at breakfast?"

"I told everyone about the Trojan War," she said.

The prince laughed! She had made him laugh and she couldn't help but notice that he looked wonderful when he laughed. And he couldn't help but notice that he told the princess the same things over and over. He was sure she thought he was stupid.

Princess Pia could not wait to see the prince. She always hurried to be with him. She didn't want to forget things that happened at breakfast. Over time, she didn't even bother to comb her hair. She was sure he thought she was ugly.

"She is lovely even when her hair is tangled," the prince thought.

"He is so smart to repeat things so I will remember," the princess thought.

"Will you marry me?" the prince asked.

"Yes!" the princess said.

Everyone was shocked when they heard the news.

No one could believe it, except, that is, for Mercury the Magician. He knew love was like that.

It seems we become most what we want to be when we are in love. But what really happens is we are loved for what we truly are.

# The Wild Swans

*Adapted by Michael P. Fertig*
*Illustrated by Kathy Mitchell*

Once there was a king who had three fine sons and a sweet daughter named Elise. The family lived happily together in a lovely castle in a small village that had been built near a great lake. Elise took care of her father and three brothers and tended to most matters around the castle.

Life was good for the family. Things were so good, in fact, that even when word reached them that an evil sorcerer had awful plans for the family, they all just laughed.

"If some evildoer wishes to get to one of us," said the king, "he'd better know that he'll have to go through all of us!"

The king's children agreed. They felt that their love for one another as a family would help to protect them through even the most difficult times.

As it happened, trouble fell on the castle that very night.

Elise tossed and turned in her bed. She was being tormented with bad dreams. She kept seeing her brothers in trouble. She didn't like the dream at all, and forced herself to wake up.

As soon as she sat up in her bed there was a knock on her door. The king came to Elise with terrible news.

"Your brothers have been taken away from us," he told her. "I know not where, but I can't stand to lose you, too."

The king told Elise to go with his most trusted servants. They would take her to safety in their home in the forest.

Elise lived hidden away in the forest for many years. In all that time, she never received word from her father, so when she was old enough, she set off in search of him and her brothers. She had no idea where to look, but she knew in her heart that they were still alive, and that they needed her help.

For several days, Elise searched for her family. She was growing desperate when she met an old woman.

"Have you seen three princes?" asked Elise.

The woman squinted in thought before finally answering.

"No, but I have seen three white swans with golden crowns on their heads," the old woman replied. She showed Elise where she had seen them.

Elise followed the old woman, but she couldn't understand why three swans might help her to find her father and brothers. This old woman must be crazy, Elise thought.

The old woman left her. Elise sat and watched the three swans. She had to admit, they were quite majestic looking with the golden coloring that circled their heads like crowns. How odd, she thought, that three different swans should have such similar markings.

The three swans flew gracefully through the air around Elise. They seemed to be waiting for something. All three would glance at the sun on the horizon and then look back toward her. Could she be imagining that these swans were actually looking at her?

Just then, as the sun was setting, Elise looked up to see the three swans as they glided down and landed beside her. In the blink of an eye the three swans changed magically into three princes. These swans were actually her brothers!

Elise was overjoyed to see them. They told her about the night they disappeared. The evil sorcerer who had threatened their whole family had managed to sneak into the castle and cast a spell on the sleeping brothers. The spell turned the brothers into swans, but only when the sun was in the sky; at night they would return to their human form. The sorcerer had also imprisoned their dear father. Elise had escaped to safety just in time.

Elise promised to do whatever she could to break the sorcerer's wicked spell. And they all vowed to find their father and free him. She sat talking to her brothers for as long into the night as she could before fatigue got the better of her and she fell asleep.

That night, a fairy came to Elise in a dream. "Only you can free your brothers," the fairy whispered. "But you must sacrifice greatly. You must craft three shirts from the petals of roses," continued the fairy. "When you cover the swans with these shirts, the spell will be broken. But you must not open your mouth to eat, drink, or speak until the shirts are made. If you do, your brothers will be swans forever."

Elise awoke with a start to find that the cave in which she slept was filled with and surrounded by hundreds of lovely rosebushes. She set to work immediately.

Elise worked day and night for thirty days. Her brothers visited her at the cave each night, and searched for their father during the day. Elise didn't dare speak to tell them what she was doing, but they understood that whatever her reason, she was doing it for them as well as their father.

Elise began to grow weaker and weaker each day. She barely had the strength to manipulate her fingers. But despite her own suffering, she dared not to eat even the tiniest morsel or drink even the smallest drop.

At long last, weak and starved, Elise completed the third shirt. Somehow, she was able summon the strength to drape the shirts over her swan brothers.

One at a time, her brothers transformed, each assuming his human form.

At that moment, Elise fell into her brothers' arms and, in a faint voice, explained how the spell had been broken. Then, too weak to continue, she closed her eyes.

Elise slept for days while her brothers nursed her back to health.

"Thank you, brothers," she said with a voice stronger than she'd had in a long time.

"No, dear sister," said the oldest of her brothers, "it is we who should be thanking you. Your sacrifice freed us from the sorcerer's spell."

"There is still more to do," she said. "We must find Father."

The brothers just smiled at her. They said nothing.

"Why do you look at me so?" she asked.

What the dream fairy had not told Elise was that her sacrifice was strong enough to rob the sorcerer of all his power. His evil could not withstand a love as great as Elise's.

"I was freed from my spell the moment your brothers were freed from theirs," said a familiar voice. It was her father!

"Father!" cried Elise. "You're here. You're alive!"

"I'm here," he said. "We're all here."

Reunited, the family lived happily ever after. And every evil sorcerer knew that to get to one of them, you had to go through all of them.

# Isabel Ant Goes to School

*Adapted by Michael P. Fertig*
*Illustrated by Richard Bernal*

Little Isabel Ant used to spend each day with her pull toy, happily playing outside in the warm summer sun. Then, as the summer days got shorter, the sun didn't feel so warm anymore.

"Summer is over," Isabel's mother told her. "That means today is your first day of school!"

Isabel had heard about school. She didn't like the idea of being cooped up inside all day long. Going to school would be strange. The idea made her feel a little nervous. Little Isabel Ant wasn't ready to go.

"Can I take my toy with me?" Isabel asked. "That might help."

"School is for children," her mother replied, "not for toys."

Little Isabel Ant tried to be brave as her mother walked her to school that day.

"I don't think school will be so bad," Mother said. "You just need to give it a chance. You might even be surprised!"

So Isabel agreed to try school for just one day.

Once she got to school and into the classroom, Isabel found that she had her very own desk. She also had never seen so many busy little ants bustling around in one place!

Their teacher, Mrs. Malinowski, gave the children a lot of things to do. Everybody got their own paper and pens, then they started to learn about reading and writing.

As the class was discussing the alphabet, something occurred to Isabel. "Ants always work together to make anthills," she said to Mrs. Malinowski. "Well, I think letters work together the same way to make words."

Mrs. Malinowski smiled. "That's right, Isabel," she said. "Very good!"

That made Isabel feel proud. As the rest of the day passed by, Isabel learned that she was pretty good at drawing and painting and counting, too!

Little Isabel Ant strolled home from school after a long day. Learning new things was fun, and reading and writing were pretty cool.

"Maybe you were right," Little Isabel Ant told her mother. "Maybe school's not so bad after all."

Isabel decided to try school for one more day. The next morning passed by quickly for her. Before she knew it, it was lunchtime!

Isabel followed the other ants to the lunchroom. They got pretty wild there, so Isabel sat off to the side, away from all the noise and commotion. It was crazy watching everyone scurry about like — well, ants!

Then Carlita the Lunch Lady called out, "Cookies and milk!"

What an even *greater* commotion that caused!

Isabel Ant squeezed her way through and got one tiny chunk of cookie. Then she knew what all the fuss was about. Carlita the Lunch Lady made the absolute best cookies Isabel had ever tasted!

At the end of the day, Isabel trotted home from school. Lunchtime had been a pleasant break, and Carlita the Lunch Lady's cookies were especially good!

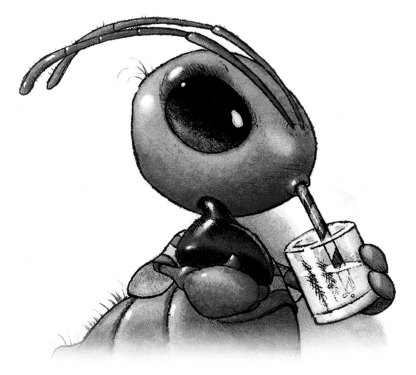

"I'm starting to think you were right, Mom," said Little Isabel Ant. "School's not really that bad at all."

Isabel thought she'd try school for another day. As soon as Isabel got there, Mrs. Malinowski said they were going to the woods for a field trip. Isabel learned about new plants and berries at every turn!

Some older children made a campfire with Mrs. Malinowski. They needed Isabel's help.

"I know how to find the best twigs!" Isabel said. She whistled for her good friend Nicoletta the Bird.

Nicoletta the Bird brought back the finest twigs in the woods. There were enough twigs to build a campfire over which each little ant could roast a marshmallow. All the children at school liked Isabel and her friend Nicoletta very much. As they sat and roasted marshmallows, they all talked and told stories. Isabel knew she was really starting to like school now.

Isabel happily hopped home from school that day. Sitting in those tiny desks was just fine as long as they had field trips and recess, too!

"I'm not totally certain yet, but it looks like you might be right, Mom," said Little Isabel Ant. "School is sort of fun."

The next day, Isabel wanted to try school again. She didn't know what to expect in school that day, but she had a hunch it might be fun.

"I wonder what will happen today," Isabel thought aloud.

Little Isabel Ant sat down at her desk. Her new friend Erin whispered to her, "Will you pretty please come to my birthday party today?"

Isabel ran home that day. Up until then, Isabel thought birthdays only happened once a year. Now she learned she could celebrate her birthday *and* her friends' birthdays, too!

Isabel had fun at Erin's party. She ate some delicious birthday cake and even got seconds!

Little Isabel Ant couldn't wait to get to school the next day. She hoped it was somebody else's birthday. She also wanted to learn how to count up to the really big numbers so she could tell how many birthday parties she might go to.

Isabel made up a new outside game for her friends that day at recess.

Isabel called the game Swing and Sing. She went first. Isabel thought of one of her favorite songs and then grabbed hold of a vine. She sang as loud as she could as she swung right around in a circle, landing safely back on the green plant.

All of Isabel's classmates loved this game. Freddy and Todd both thought Isabel was so much fun, and Jamie and Gladys loved to hear her sing. They looked up to Little Isabel Ant as the most adventurous ant in their class.

"You're the best, Isabel!" the children shouted.

Little Isabel Ant rushed home from school after another fun day. She was so excited.

"You were absolutely right, Mom," said Little Isabel Ant. "School's not bad at all. In fact, it's great!"

Little Isabel Ant never dreaded going to another day of school. She loved it so much she was even sad when school was out for the summer.

But just a little.

# The Elves and the Shoemaker

*Adapted by Michael P. Fertig*
*Illustrated by Kristen Goeters*

For many years, there was a small shoe shop that flourished in a village known for its good taste in clothing. Times were very good for the people of the village, so they had extra money to spend on lavish clothes and fancy shoes. This made for a very well-dressed town. But more than that, times were especially good for the town's humble shoemaker and his wife. They lived quite comfortably making shoes for the village.

The villagers loved the shoes that the shoemaker and his wife would make. No two pairs were alike. Everyone owned their own unique pair. But what people *really* loved, besides the fact that every pair of shoes was more beautiful than the last, was that every pair of shoes was so well made. One pair could last a person half a lifetime.

However, like so many good things that we read about in stories, the good times in the village began to fade. The crops from the surrounding farms began to yield less product for the farmers to sell. This meant they made less money. Since they made less money, they had less to spend on supplies in town. Since fewer supplies in town were being sold, the supply store owners had fewer jobs to give to people. Since there were fewer jobs, fewer people stayed to live in the village. Over time, many of the villagers found themselves very poor.

The shoemaker was one of these people. At first he thought that he and his wife would be fine. Everyone needs shoes, he thought. But what he forgot was that he had already sold everyone shoes—shoes that were sure to last a long, long time. Times became tough for the shoemaker and his wife.

When winter arrived, the poor shoemaker and his wife discovered that they had only enough leather left to make one pair of shoes. After the leather was gone, they would have no way to make a living, for they could not afford any more.

"Things will work out," said the shoemaker. "Things always tend to work out." He cut out the leather and went to bed, planning to finish the shoes the next day.

In the morning, instead of the pieces of leather, the shoemaker found a marvelous pair of shoes! The shoes were beautifully made, with fantastic detail. "Who could have made these?" he wondered, amazed.

As luck would have it, a man from the big city happened to be traveling through the village that day. The rich tourist came into the shoemaker's shop.

"I've just managed to step into a magnificent puddle of sludge, and I simply cannot walk around in these muddy shoes," he said. "Do you have anything in my size?"

The shoemaker and his wife showed him the mysterious shoes. They fit perfectly!

"These are the loveliest shoes I have ever seen!" exclaimed the traveler. He gave the shoemaker a gold coin to pay for them.

With the gold coin, the poor shoemaker was able to buy enough leather to make *two* pairs of shoes. Once again the shoemaker cut the leather and placed the pieces on his workbench.

The next morning he found two more pairs of finished shoes. "How is this happening?" the shoemaker asked his wife.

As luck would have it once again, the tourist who had come into the shop the day before had told his wife and her sister about the fine shoes. They made a special trip to the shop.

The shoemaker could hardly believe that the two brand-new pairs of shoes fit the ladies perfectly.

"Never have we seen shoes like this!" the women squealed in delight. The sisters paid handsomely for their new footwear.

This continued for many nights. The shoemaker would go to bed and awake to find shoes on his workbench. Every day people would come in and buy the exact shoes that had just been made. Eventually, the shoemaker's shelves were filled with beautiful shoes like no one had ever seen before.

Word of the shoemaker's fine shoes soon made him the most popular shoemaker for miles around. So popular was his shoe shop that the entire village began to make money from the people coming for shoes. But still something bothered him. One evening he said to his wife, "Every night, someone works hard to help us. It's a shame we don't even know who it is. Why don't we stay up to find out?"

That night, just like always, the shoemaker cut leather into pieces and placed them on his workbench. But instead of going to bed, he and his wife hid in the doorway.

Soon, to the astonishment of the shoemaker and his wife, two elves suddenly appeared on the workbench! Their clothes were old and ragged, so full of holes and rips that the elves must have been quite cold. Nevertheless, they worked happily all through the night.

The shoemaker and his wife tiptoed up the stairs to bed. The next morning they talked in disbelief about what they had seen. They both thought it remarkable that two elves had chosen to help them. But of course, being the kind couple that they were, the shoemaker and his wife couldn't help but notice the state of the elves' clothes.

"Clearly they are in great need of new clothes themselves," said the shoemaker, "yet they work all night to help us."

The shoemaker's wife had an idea. "Let's make those little elves the clothes they need!" she said. That evening, instead of leaving leather on the bench, they left tiny new clothes and shoes.

Once again hidden in the shadows, the shoemaker and his wife watched as the elves magically appeared at midnight. They climbed upon the workbench and saw the two tiny suits. Their little faces brightened and they shouted gleefully. They immediately threw on the fine new suits and shoes. They were so excited that they began to dance and sing.

After that night, the elves never came back. But the shoemaker and his wife did not mind. They were thankful for the help of the elves and were glad they could return the favor.

The shoemaker's success had helped the village to flourish again. Everyone in town was thankful for this. But no one was more thankful than the shoemaker and his wife for the kindness of those two little strangers.

# The North Wind

*Adapted by Lisa Harkrader*
*Illustrated by Beth Foster Wiggins*

Nate had just started his walk back home. He had been in the village buying some oats for dinner. His mother had given him a few coins to buy the oats. Thankfully, they weren't that expensive and he still had coins left.

However, on the way home the North Wind began to blow. He blew right into Nate's basket, sending all of the oats across the field. The North Wind blew and blew until the oats were completely gone.

Nate stared at the empty basket. "I can't go home without oats for our dinner," he thought to himself, so he returned to the village and bought more oats.

On the way home the North Wind began to blow again. He blew right into Nate's basket, sending all of the oats across the field. Nate watched, dumbstruck, as the wind blew until the oats were completely gone.

Once more, Nate returned to the village, and once more, he bought a basket of oats.

But sure enough, as he walked home the North Wind began to blow. To make a long story short, Nate's oats were gone, leaving him with an empty basket and no more money.

"I have no choice," Nate said out loud. "I have to go home without oats."

Nate went to bed hungry that night. He knew his mother was hungry, too. He woke early the next morning and knew what he had to do.

"I must find the North Wind," he said. "I must see if he'll give us back our oats."

Nate walked through the dark and cold morning until he finally came to a house.

This house had to belong to the North Wind. Nate knocked at the door. It squeaked open and a giant, wrinkled face peeked out. Sure enough, it was the North Wind.

"Yes? What is it?" whooshed the North Wind.

"Three times I bought oats, sir," began Nate, "and three times you blew them away. I came here to get my oats."

"I don't have your oats," said the North Wind. "It is my job to blow the wind. Once I blow oats away, they are gone, scattered across the fields. But you were brave to come here. I will reward you and give you this instead."

The North Wind handed Nate a tablecloth.

"Say the words, 'Cloth! Cloth! Serve food!' and you will never be hungry again," the North Wind said.

Nate thanked the North Wind and set out for home. As it was growing late, he stopped at an inn for dinner and sat down in the dining room. He spread the cloth on the dinner table.

"Cloth! Cloth! Serve food!"

A roast beef sprang from the cloth, followed by potatoes, carrots, and cake. The innkeeper stood watching and smiled. He offered Nate the very best room in the inn.

The next morning, Nate ran all the way home. He burst into his cottage and spread the cloth on the table.

"Mother, look what I have," he said. "Cloth! Cloth! Serve food!"

Nate waited. His mother, unsure of what she was supposed to be looking at, watched as nothing happened.

Nate ran his hands over the tablecloth. He smoothed out the wrinkles.

"Cloth! Cloth! Serve food!" he said.

Still, nothing happened.

"I don't get it," Nate said. "It worked at the inn. The innkeeper saw it. He could tell you."

That afternoon, Nate set back out to find the North Wind. He walked through the darkest part of the forest until he came to the house made of stones. Nate knocked at the door. It squeaked

open as the North Wind peeked out.

"Yes? What is it now?" whooshed the North Wind.

Nate handed the tablecloth to the North Wind and said, "It doesn't work! You tricked me."

"Why would I trick you?" he asked. "I blow the wind. I do not have time for tricks."

"The cloth doesn't work," Nate said.

"This isn't the cloth I gave you," said the North Wind. "This one is torn and stained. But once again, you were brave to come here, so I'll reward you by giving you this instead."

93

The North Wind gave Nate a piggy bank.

"Say the words, 'Bank! Bank! Make money!' and you will never be poor again," the North Wind said.

Nate thanked the North Wind and set out for home. It was getting late, so Nate stopped at the same inn for the night.

"Bank! Bank! Make money," he said.

Coins dropped from the bank as the innkeeper watched and smiled. Nate gave the innkeeper the coins to pay for a room. He gave Nate the very best room.

The next morning, Nate ran home.

"Mother, look!" he said. "Bank! Bank! Make money."

Once again nothing happened. Nate rubbed his hands over the piggy bank.

"Bank! Bank! Make money!" he said again. The bank still did nothing.

"I think you have been tricked," his mother said.

So for a third time, Nate set out to find the North Wind. He knocked at the door and once again the North Wind peeked out.

"You *again!*" whooshed the North Wind. "What is it this time?"

Nate handed the piggy bank to the North Wind. "You tricked me again," he said.

"Young man, I did not trick you," he said. "I blow the wind. I don't have time for tricks. Besides, this isn't the bank I gave you. This bank is chipped and cracked."

"Oh, no," said Nate. "It must have been the innkeeper." Nate was upset.

"You are a brave lad," the North Wind said, "so I have something that you can use against tricksters."

He handed Nate a rope.

"Say the words, 'Rope! Rope! Tie him up!' and you'll never be tricked again," he said.

"Thank you," Nate said. "You have been very kind to me."

He set off for the inn with the magic rope. When the innkeeper saw Nate come in with a rope, he smiled and gave Nate the very best room. Nate set the rope on a chair, crawled into bed, and waited. The door squeaked open in the middle of the night as the innkeeper slipped into the room looking for the rope. Nate sprang from his bed.

"Rope! Rope! Tie him up!" he said.

The rope slithered around the innkeeper.

"Let me go!" the innkeeper said.

"After you give back my tablecloth and my bank," Nate said.

The innkeeper told Nate where to find his things. Then Nate untied the innkeeper.

Nate ran all the way home.

"Mother! I got the North Wind's gifts back! Look!" he said. "Cloth! Cloth! Serve food! Bank! Bank! Make money!"

Nate's mother watched as a pot of stew sprang up from the cloth and coins spilled from the bank. A tear rolled from her eye as she realized what this meant. She and her son would never be hungry or poor again.

"Now let's eat," said Nate. "I'm famished."

# The End